For everyone big or small,
for the child who lives within us all.
These words were sent to comfort you.
Take time to read them. You'll know what to do.

Dedicated to the memory of Stella Heslip,
A.K.A. Boots Clute. Thank you for the inspiration.
I can hear you now. ♥

With immense gratitude, I would like to acknowledge
the support of Terry, Sammy and Mags.
Thanks for your editing, photography
and endless "listening with love".
I will always love you!

I Will Always Love you

Written by Melissa Lyons
Illustrated by Mary Cindrich

If you're reading this now and I'm far away,
please pay attention, I've got something to say.

It was my time to go
and I can't explain why.

But there was a reason.
It was my turn to fly.

Now I can see you from my new place of rest.
You must understand you are still truly blessed.

Realize that by letting me go,
you'll give us both freedom, more than you know.

Believe in angels and spirits or not,
but consider this, I hear all of your thoughts.

Your life lies ahead and it's all very great.
I'm privileged now to see all of your fate.

I have one last wish and it's part of a theme.

It's you choosing to choose to follow your dream.

My gifts to you include memories and love,
and now you'll have more with my guidance above.

I'll send you hints so you know I'm around,
Pay closer attention to each sight and each sound.

You might see butterflies or other clues that I leave.
It could be a rainbow, you'll just have to believe.

Focus on love and trust in good things.
Listen to your intuition and see what life brings.

Open your mind and change as you need.
Embrace new directions; see where they lead.

Welcome your challenges as they appear.
Accept them as lessons; there's nothing to fear.

They come with messages and purposes too.
It's all part of your learning; they're gifts for you.

See them with gratitude and understand their role;

then get back to focusing the thoughts you control.

Trust your heart as you follow your dreams.
It has been directed by the highest of teams.

You hold the power and the answers inside.
Turn into your heart; let it be your guide.

You create your world with each thought that you think.
Your beliefs build your future as fast as you blink.

The mind is a garden that grows flowers and weeds.
One who chooses good thoughts always succeeds.

Trust me I know, advice is easy to give.
But divine wisdom shows, this is how you should live.

Be the one who shares the light that was mine.
Honor me now by letting yours shine.

Trust that I'm free and home at last.
Cherish each moment, life goes by so fast.

And remember...

I Will Always love you

Second Edition 2017
Printed in China
ISBN 978-0-9959491-0-2